NOTE TO PARENTS

Based on the beloved Walt Disney motion picture *Peter Pan,* this book focuses on what happens when evil Captain Hook captures Peter's friend Tiger Lily. Tiger Lily knows something that could place Peter in danger. Despite the pirate's threats, she bravely refuses to tell.

When Peter sees Captain Hook trying to harm his friend, he bravely flies to the rescue. He does not hesitate to fight, even though the captain is bigger *and* has a bigger sword. Peter's bravery and fast thinking have a good result—the captain runs away. Even better, Peter's new friend Wendy has learned that it is right to be brave when danger threatens us or our friends.

This book recounts one memorable episode from the movie that will help children learn an important lesson about the value of bravery.

PETER PAN

Saves the Day

A BOOK ABOUT BRAVERY

A GOLDEN BOOK • NEW YORK
Western Publishing Company, Inc., Racine, Wisconsin 53404

Once upon a time, in a magical place called Never Land, there lived a boy named Peter Pan. Peter could fly, and he had many wonderful adventures with his friends—Tinker Bell the pixie, the mermaids in the lagoon, and the Lost Boys. One of Peter's best friends was Tiger Lily, the Indian princess.

Peter's only enemy was the terrible pirate Captain Hook. The captain hated Peter Pan. It was during a fight with Peter that Hook lost his hand to a hungry crocodile. That was why he had to wear a hook.

The crocodile had liked the taste of Hook's hand, and it followed the captain everywhere, trying to get the rest of him. Captain Hook lived in constant fear of the crocodile—and in constant hope of getting even with Peter Pan.

One day Hook was plotting with his first mate, Smee. Hook said, "I have a plan. I'll capture that Indian princess and force her to tell me the location of Peter Pan's secret hiding place. Then I'll sneak up on Pan and get rid of the pesky brat once and for all!"

Just then, the lookout called to Captain Hook, "Pan above the starboard bow!"

Peter Pan was flying overhead with Tinker Bell and his new friends, Wendy, Michael, and John.

"Fire the cannon and blast them out of the sky!" Captain Hook commanded his crew.

But Peter saw the cannonball coming and acted quickly to protect his friends.

"Tink, lead Wendy, Michael, and John to the secret hiding place while I draw Hook's fire," Peter told the pixie. "You'll be safe there," he assured the children.

"But what about you?" Wendy asked.

"I'm not afraid," Peter declared boldly. With that, he called down to the pirate, "You'll never catch me!"

The captain shook his hook in the air and shouted, "I'll get you, Pan, if it's the last thing I do!"

As his friends flew to safety Peter dodged the cannonballs.
He flew so fast that none of the shots came near him. Peter
Pan's laughter rang out over the booming cannon.

"Pan will sing a different tune when Tiger Lily tells me where his hiding place is," the captain told Smee. He ordered his men to stop firing the cannon.

Then he and Smee rowed to shore to capture the Indian princess.

Tiger Lily was walking through the woods. She heard
a twig snap behind her. She stopped, then took a few more
steps.

Suddenly Hook and Smee sprang from the bushes where they had been hiding. They grabbed Tiger Lily. She kicked and struggled, but she couldn't get away.

"Tell me where Peter Pan's hiding place is, and I will set you free," Hook hissed.

Tiger Lily shook her head. She would never reveal Peter's secret hiding place.

Hook stamped his foot. "We'll see about that," he said. He and Smee tied Tiger Lily's arms and legs with thick ropes. They carried her to their boat and rowed to Skull Rock, a huge hollow place that filled with water when the tide came in.

Peter Pan was showing Wendy the mermaid lagoon when he heard Hook's menacing voice. He peered around a rock and gasped. "It's Tiger Lily—with Hook and Smee!" he said. "Tiger Lily is in trouble! Come on, Wendy!"

"But, Peter, it's dangerous," Wendy said. "I'm afraid!"

"We have to be brave, Wendy," said Peter. "Tiger Lily is in trouble, and we must rescue her."

Inside Skull Rock the captain and Smee tied Tiger Lily to a rock in the water.

"Where is Pan's hiding place?" Hook demanded.

The princess bravely kept silent.

"Tell or drown," Captain Hook said angrily. "The tide is coming in."

Water began to fill the stone skull. It soaked Tiger Lily's ankles and swirled up her legs. A shivering chill ran up her spine, but still she would not tell her friend's secret.

Then a strange ghostly voice echoed through the rock. "Untie the princess or else!" it warned.

Smee shook in his boots while the captain followed the sound of the voice. He climbed from rock to rock until he found...

Peter Pan crouched behind a rock, talking in his deepest voice and muffling the sound with his hat.

"Aha!" Hook shouted. He saw that Peter Pan had only a small knife. He drew his great sword.

"Fight me if you dare!" Peter said.

Soon Skull Rock was filled with the clanging of knife against sword. Up and down the slippery stones Captain Hook chased Peter Pan. At last he cornered Peter at the edge of a cliff.

"Victory is mine!" Hook shouted, lunging at Peter with his long sword.

Peter Pan jumped aside just in time. The pirate fell off the ledge and into the water with a great splash.

And there, eyes bulging above the water, was the terrible crocodile!

"Save me, Smee!" the captain shrieked.

Smee grabbed Hook's arm and pulled him into the rowboat.

"Row! Row! Row the boat!" the pirate shouted as the crocodile chased their small rowboat out the mouth of Skull Rock.

Peter untied Tiger Lily. For a moment Peter, Wendy, and
Tiger Lily laughed at the frightened pirate. Then the three
friends flew to the Indian camp where Tiger Lily lived.

When the Indian chief heard how Peter Pan had rescued his daughter, he presented Peter with a beautiful feathered headdress.

"Now you are a brave," the chief declared. "We will call you Chief Little Flying Eagle."

"Peter, you really are brave," Wendy said. "You stand up for yourself, and you stand up for your friends. You fight back when someone tries to harm you *or* them."

"Tiger Lily is brave, too," Peter said. "She wouldn't tell my secret, no matter what."

Tiger Lily nodded. "It's not easy to be brave," she thought.
"But it helps if you know you're doing the right thing." And she
joined all her friends in a big celebration.